Peppa's Pizza Party

Adapted by Rebecca Potters

This book is based on the TV series *Peppa Pig*. *Peppa Pig* is created by Neville Astley and Mark Baker.
Peppa Pig © Astley Baker Davies Ltd/Entertainment One UK Ltd 2003.

ISBN 978-1-338-61170-0

10 9 8 7 6   22 23 24
Printed in the U.S.A.   40

First printing 2020

www.peppapig.com

SCHOLASTIC INC.

It is lunchtime at
Peppa's house.
"Can we make
pizzas?" Peppa asks.
George loves
pizza! So do
Mummy and
Daddy Pig.

Peppa is excited to start. But first, everyone must wash their hands. They use soap and water to get all clean!

When they are done washing, they gather ingredients.
"To make our pizzas," Daddy Pig says, "We need flour, ..."
"Tomato," chimes in Mummy Pig.
"Cheese," continues Daddy Pig, "and toppings."

But wait! There's something missing.
"George likes pineapple on his pizza," Peppa says.

"Pineapple?" Daddy Pig repeats. "On *pizza*?
I think that's against the law!"

"Hee! Hee! Hee!" Peppa laughs.

Daddy Pig is being silly. It is not against the law to put pineapple on pizza.

Now it is time to make the pizzas!
Mummy Pig puts the flour into a bowl. Then she adds
water. This mixture will become pizza dough. Tasty!

Mummy Pig sprinkles a little flour on the table so that the dough doesn't stick.

Then, with their clean hands,
Peppa and George knead the dough.
Bam! Bam! Bam!

"I am big and strong!" Peppa says.
"And George is big and strong, too."

Next, they make the dough into four balls. These will become four pizza pies.

Mummy Pig rolls the dough balls flat with her rolling pin. "Oh!" says Peppa. "They look like pizzas now!"

Mummy and Daddy Pig make a sauce with the tomatoes. Then, Peppa and George smooth it over the dough.

"I like making pizza, *snort!*" Peppa says. "It's so fun!"

Now it is time to decorate the pizzas!

"Can we make happy faces on top?" Peppa asks.

"Of course we can!" replies Daddy Pig. "I'll use mushrooms to make eyes, and olives for the smile . . ."

"And I'll use onions for the eyes and basil for the smile," says Mummy Pig.

Peppa uses sweetcorn for the smile and little tomatoes for the eyes.

George has pineapple for the eyes and cheese for the smile!

Mummy Pig puts on her oven mitts. Then, she places the pizzas in the oven to bake.

When the pizzas are done,
Peppa, George, Mummy Pig, and
Daddy Pig eat in the garden.
Their pizzas are very good.
"These are the best pizzas in
the world!" says Peppa.

Peppa loves pizza.
Everyone loves pizza!

Decorate your own pizza by using the stickers on the next page! Just remember, don't eat these stickers!